Alison Hutchison

Series editor
ALISTAIR
BRYCE-CLEGG

fantastic ideas for
exploring shape and pattern

FEATHERSTONE

FEATHERSTONE
Bloomsbury Publishing Plc
50 Bedford Square, London, WC1B 3DP, UK

BLOOMSBURY, FEATHERSTONE and the Feather logo are trademarks of Bloomsbury Publishing Plc

First published in Great Britain 2019 by Bloomsbury Publishing Plc

A catalogue record for this book is available from the British Library

ISBN: PB: 978-1-4729-6454-0; ePDF: 978-1-4729-6456-4

2 4 6 8 10 9 7 5 3 1

Series design: Lynda Murray

Printed and bound in India by Replika Press Pvt. Ltd.

To find out more about our authors and books visit www.bloomsbury.com and sign up for our newsletters

Contents

Introduction

As they grow up, children quickly discover that shapes can move and change, can have texture, temperature, weight, scent and sound, or indeed none of these attributes. They learn that shapes can be held, squashed, stacked and thrown, that the same shape can be found in all manner of sizes and forms. They notice and observe patterns all around them – in humans, in everyday rhythms, in nature and in play. The dynamic, stimulating world of shape and pattern is all around us to observe and explore from birth.

There is a wonderfully rich array of common shapes and patterns to explore and investigate, to share and to wonder about. Yet, in the early years, we often narrow this entirely to asking children to recall the names of some basic shapes and using relatively uninteresting materials to copy and continue a pattern. If we narrow down shape and pattern to these experiences and lose breadth and depth, we squander children's interest and any connection to the real world.

The ideas within this book aim to widen children's experience of shape and pattern, and to take a broad, creative approach to learning. They will provide stimulating contexts in which children can engage with and explore characteristics of shape and pattern while handling and using a range of everyday and play objects, as well as taking learning forward with simple mathematical materials.

The activities target specific areas of learning within shape and pattern. Children will have the opportunity to use shape names, become familiar with characteristics of different flat and solid shapes, and recognise, describe, copy and continue patterns. However, they will do so in contexts aimed at stimulating thinking, that can be explored holistically, and that give scope for children to take the lead, make choices and follow their interests. This enables children to access concepts at their individual stage of development.

Each idea and the accompanying 'Taking it forward' suggestions have been successfully used in a range of settings. I hope that you enjoy putting them into practice. I would also encourage you to use them as a springboard – adapt them to your setting, to the materials that you have available and to meet the needs and interests of the children that you are planning for. Let's ignite discovery and wonder in this fascinating area of mathematics.

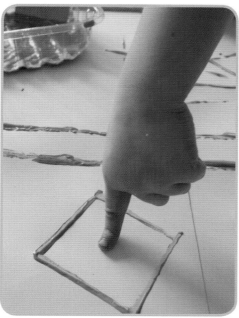

The structure of the book

Before you start any activity, read through everything on the page so you are familiar with the whole activity and what you might need to plan in advance. The pages are all organised in the same way.

What you need lists the resources required for the activity. These are likely to be readily available in most settings or can be bought or made easily.

Top tips give a brief word of advice or helpful tip that could make all the difference to the experience of the activity for you and your children.

What to do tells you step by step what you need to do to complete the activity.

The **Health & Safety** tips are often obvious, but safety can't be overstressed. In many cases there are no specific hazards involved in completing the activity, and your usual health and safety measures should be enough. In others there are particular issues to be noted and addressed.

What's in it for the children? tells you (and others) briefly how the suggested activities contribute to learning.

Finally, **Taking it forward** gives ideas for additional activities on the same theme, or for developing the activity further. These will be particularly useful for things that have gone especially well or where children show a real interest. In many cases they use the same resources, and in every case they have been designed to extend learning and broaden the children's experiences.

Puzzle pieces

2D shape

What you need:

- Craft knife
- Ruler
- Large sheets of sturdy card
- A large plate
- Shallow basket or tray

Top tip

Do not limit the children to simply recreating regular shapes with these materials. Imaginative, open-ended exploration is valuable as the children will independently create multiple shapes as they explore, particularly if they are working together.

What's in it for the children?

This is an opportunity to use straight lines, angles and curves to create regular shapes, focusing thinking on the idea that shapes are a series of lines and curves joined together in different ways.

Taking it forward

- Working together, ask the children to challenge each other to use the materials to create specific shapes or representations of objects.

- Replace these materials with branches and twigs, using them in the same way.

What to do:

1. Use a craft knife and ruler to cut sturdy card into a selection of straight strips of different lengths and curves of different diameters, as well as angled and right-angled corners. Draw around a large plate to create the curved pieces.

2. Gather the card pieces into a shallow basket or tray that will be accessible to a small group of children.

3. Take time at this point to ensure that the card pieces can be used to satisfactorily create different shapes and images of objects. Adjust and recreate the shapes as necessary.

4. Offer the materials to the children. Invite them to make shapes, pictures and scenes with the shapes.

5. Allow lots of time for independent investigation, exploration and open-ended imaginative use as well as focused shape work.

Straight lines
2D shape

What you need:

- Sturdy card
- Scissors
- Paint
- Shallow trays
- Paper

Top tip ⭐

Ensure the card is sturdy and regularly replaced as and when it becomes saturated with paint. Reusing packing boxes works well.

What's in it for the children?

This is a great way for children to experience joining or bringing together several lines to create different shape outlines. This essentially begins the journey of knowing and understanding that all shapes are created when several lines come together to make an enclosed space.

Taking it forward

- Provide drawing materials and access to rulers. Demonstrate how to use the ruler to create a straight line and incorporate rulers into your provision.

- Link this activity to developing scissor skills. Use the resources to print straight lines and, once dry, invite children to cut along the lines.

What to do:

1. Cut the sturdy card into easy-to-handle strips, approximately 8 cm long and 5 cm wide.

2. Put some paint in shallow trays. Model how to dip the edge of the card strip into the paint and then use it to print a straight line onto the paper.

3. Continue to print with the card strip while the children observe.

4. Model different possibilities. For example, create a long straight line, a series of joined lines to create a pathway or maze, representations of regular flat shapes or everyday objects.

5. Provide each child with a shallow tray filled with paint, one strip of card and access to plain paper.

6. Encourage the children to use the resources to explore making different lines, shapes, patterns and pictures as shown in your demonstration.

Play scenes

What you need:

- Large floor space
- Masking tape
- Vehicles
- Set of small wooden blocks or similar from provision

What's in it for the children?

This is an opportunity to discover, reinforce or extend knowledge of the square shape through play. Building on top of the masking tape lines to lift the squares emphasises the outline of each shape and furthers the experience from flat to solid.

Taking it forward

- Use large sheets of paper and drawing materials to create a similar road map. Rolls of paper work well.

- Use this experience to introduce the concept of a maze.

- Create a similar scene with natural materials and small world materials in tuff trays, using shapes and lines to define different areas.

What to do:

1. Create a large square area for vehicle play. Use masking tape to mark 1.5 m² or 2 m² of floor space.

2. Within the square, create different-sized smaller squares using the masking tape.

3. Invite the children to use the squared play area with the vehicles as they would a playmat or play scene.

4. Talk with the children as they play. Ask: 'I can see lots of the same shape here, do you know the name of these shapes?, How would you describe this shape?, Can you draw one in the air using your finger?'

5. Offer play alternatives, e.g. 'Are these squares water? Can I drive in them? Perhaps we could use the squares as parking spaces or garages. What do you think?'

6. Introduce the wooden blocks into the play and use them to build on top of the masking tape lines, creating a 3D playscape.

7. At the end of the session, clear away the masking tape, vehicles and blocks.

8. In the next session, offer the unprepared materials to the children. Challenge them to create their own 'road mat' or town, providing adult assistance with the masking tape if required.

9. Ask the children to think about which shapes they are going to use and the size of the shapes. Give them plenty of time to create and play.

Who am I?
2D shape

What you need:

- Whiteboard

Top tip ⭐

This is a brilliant activity to share with caregivers; paper can replace the whiteboard.

What's in it for the children?

This engaging adult-led game focuses on recognising shapes and their attributes. It can be used to introduce, consolidate or secure recognition of 2D or 3D shapes depending on the intended learning.

Taking it forward

- Begin with only a few shapes on the whiteboard, increasing them as children's knowledge and confidence grows.

- Invite individual children to take the adult role, with support as required.

- Provide the children with individual whiteboards. Have each child draw their chosen shape after listening to all three clues and reveal their boards when you ask 'Who am I?'

- Play the game without the visual reference of drawings on the whiteboard.

What to do:

1. Identify the shapes that you will focus on during this activity based on the group's current experience, understanding and knowledge gaps.

2. Begin by drawing five or six regular shapes on the whiteboard.

3. Gather a group of children together; explain that you are going to use the shapes to play a game of 'Who Am I?'

4. Select one of shapes without revealing this to the children.

5. Give three clues to guide them to identify your chosen shape. Begin each clue with the words 'I am…', e.g. 'I am a shape with four sides' and 'I am the same shape as a wheel'. It may be worthwhile preparing some clues for each shape beforehand to ensure the activity has breadth and flow.

6. Recap the clues and invite the children to guess your chosen shape.

7. Repeat for all of the different shapes on the board.

Make me

2D shape

What you need:

- **Photographs of everyday objects**
- **Sturdy plain card**
- **Set of small 2D shapes**

Top tip ⭐

Take time to work through a few photographs beforehand and check whether the shapes provided are up to the task of recreating images satisfactorily – otherwise, this may become a frustrating activity.

What's in it for the children?

This activity focuses children on the overall shape of the object in the photograph. They must select appropriate 2D shapes to adequately represent the solid image. It is also necessary for them to break a larger object down into different individual shapes.

Taking it forward

- Have the children work in pairs. One child can describe the photograph and the other must build the model without a visual aid for support.

- Increase the challenge by asking the children to make the object within the picture using as few shapes as possible.

What to do:

1. Gather together a set of photographs of everyday things: animals, food, vehicles, nature, objects from within a home all work well.

2. Mount the photographs onto sturdy card approximately 10 cm by 5 cm. You may wish to laminate the cards at this point to make them last longer.

3. Present the cards face down along with access to the 2D shapes.

4. Invite children to select one card at a time and to use the 2D shapes to create a picture of the image on the card.

Dough shapes
2D shape

What you need:

- Salt dough
- Rollers
- Rolling cutters
- Set of 2D shapes

Top tip

Provide each child with a relatively large ball of dough.

What to do:

1. Organise a large ball of salt dough, a roller and a rolling cutter for each child.

2. Ensure that that the 2D shapes are within easy reach of each child's working area.

3. Challenge the children to cut as many different shapes as they can out of their dough using rolling cutters.

4. Encourage them to compare the 2D shapes provided to their cut shapes.

5. Take time to work alongside the children, prompting use of shape-related language as they identify and cut each shape.

6. Make statements as you observe the children at work, e.g. 'I thought you were cutting a square but you have cut two long sides and two shorter so it can't be a square.'

What's in it for the children?

This is an opportunity to focus on the different properties of regular 2D shapes through recreating them out of dough. Working alongside the children during this activity will provide many opportunities to introduce, use and reinforce shape-related language (e.g. side, corner, straight, curved), as well as size-related language (e.g. long and short), and directional and positional language (e.g. beside, along, from, top, bottom, up, down, end, beginning).

Taking it forward

- Use this activity to focus entirely on one shape, challenging the children to cut as many of that one shape as they can from their ball of dough within a set time.

- Provide biscuit dough rather than salt dough and bake the cut shapes for snack time or for the children to take home to share with parents/carers.

- Replace the rolling cutters with child-safe knives or provide both.

Icing pens

2D shape

What you need:

- One plain plate per child
- Icing pens
- Examples of regular 2D shapes
- Wipes or damp sponges

Top tip

You may wish to explore the use of icing pens as a drawing tool before they are used in this context. Young children are always very tempted to taste foodstuff. Pre-empt this, discuss and be clear in your discouragement of 'tasting' before the activity begins.

What to do:

1. Provide each child with a plate and access to the icing pens.

2. Use the sample shapes throughout this adult-led activity.

3. Focus on one shape at a time; show the shape, name the shape, describe the shape – pointing to each feature.

4. Invite each child to use an icing pen to draw the shape on their plate. Allow time for a few attempts.

5. Compare the shapes, celebrate success and reinforce descriptions of each shape.

6. Ask the children to use a wipe or sponge to clean their plate after each shape, ready for the next.

Health & Safety

Though this is not a tasting experience, be allergy aware.

What's in it for the children?

A fun alternative to wipe-clean whiteboards, this activity offers a similar non-permanent surface to encourage even the most reluctant children to attempt to draw shapes. The adult direction in this activity and focus on one shape at a time makes it a great context for less-experienced learners or for use as an introduction to accurately drawing a representation of each shape.

Taking it forward

- Use this engaging context to introduce less familiar 2D shapes such as kite, diamond, hexagon, pentagon.

- To increase the challenge, lead this activity without any visual reference to the shapes; simply name a shape and invite the children to draw it.

- For further challenge, replace shape names with descriptions, inviting the children to draw from these, e.g. 'I would like you to draw a shape with four straight sides.'

Magnetic makes

What you need:

- Wooden lollipop sticks
- Magnetic dots
- Storage container
- Magnetic board or surface

What to do:

1. Taking each lollipop stick, attach a magnetic dot to each end of one side.
2. Gather the lollipop sticks together in a container.
3. Offer the sticks alongside the magnetic board for independent use.
4. Allow the children time to create lines, shapes, pictures and patterns with the sticks.

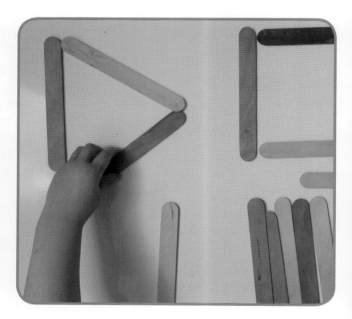

What's in it for the children?

The magnetic sticks offer an opportunity to independently create with a simple material that is easy to handle.

Taking it forward

- Offer a selection of magnetic sticks of different lengths to widen the possibilities.
- Invite the children to challenge each other to create different shapes or images of everyday objects.

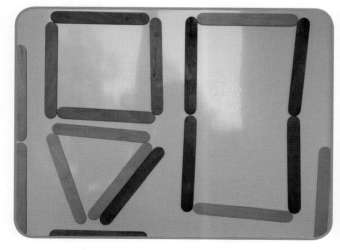

Shape reveal

2D shape

What you need:

- Plain black construction paper
- Scissors
- Plain black card, A5
- Plain white card, A5
- Sticky tape

Top tip

Using sticky tape to attach the shapes to the cards rather than glue enables shapes to be swapped between cards. Make a set of four cards and rotate the shapes.

What's in it for the children?

This is a fun, tactile opportunity to focus on developing 2D shape recognition and identification.

Taking it forward

- Provide the materials and invite the children to create their own shape reveal cards. To simplify the process, they could draw the shape rather than cut it from paper.

- Create shape silhouette jigsaws, cutting whole shapes from card and then into segments for the children to reform.

What to do:

1. Cut different 2D shapes from plain black construction paper; these shapes will be 'revealed' during the activity.

2. To make each 'shape reveal' card, fold a sheet of black card into equal quarters and cut along the folds into four pieces.

3. Take a piece of white card and place the four black card pieces on top so that they completely cover the card.

4. Using sticky tape, attach the black pieces one a time to the outside top and bottom edges of the card, so that they create four flaps that can be lifted one at a time.

5. Attach the 2D shapes onto the centre of the white cards, one per card, using a section of rolled up sticky tape to secure.

6. Gather the children together and share one of the cards, showing them how to carefully lift one black flap at a time, revealing different parts of the shape.

7. Explain that the objective of this activity is to guess the name of the shape being revealed as each flap is lifted.

8. Offer the cards to the children for exploration either independently or with others.

Copy me
2D shape

What you need:

- Identical sets of regular 2D shapes
- A small screen or barrier; this can be either a cardboard box or DIY card screen

Top tip

This activity also works well as an adult versus larger group of children game. How close can you get to creating their picture? Children love it when this is a challenge for an adult and it offers less confident learners the safe context of a group to work within.

What's in it for the children?

While describing the picture to a partner, children must use accurate shape names and positional vocabulary if their partner is to correctly replicate the picture. It is a real challenge for children to listen to a description, select and place the correct corresponding shapes to replicate a picture without a visual reference.

Taking it forward

- As a lead-in to this activity, use the shapes to create picture cards for children to recreate.
- As an individual activity, invite children to use the shapes to create a picture then take a photograph before disassembling.
- Try this activity with whiteboards and magnetic shapes.

What to do:

1. Give each child an identical set of 2D shapes and ask them to get into pairs.

2. Position the children at a table or in a floor space so they cannot see each other. You could use a cardboard box or card screen to create a barrier, though they must be close enough so that they can talk and listen to each other throughout the activity. Alternatively, ask them to sit back to back.

3. Explain that one child is going to use their shapes to create a picture while the other child waits.

4. Invite one child to create a picture using their set of shapes. The other child must not be able to see this.

5. Ask the first child to describe their picture while their partner uses their shapes to attempt to copy it exactly.

6. Allow lots of time for the children to describe, discuss and question together.

7. Explain to the children that when they think they have the same picture, they can look at each other's creations to compare.

8. The children then swap roles and repeat the activity.

Chalk outlines
2D shape

What you need:

- Jumbo chalks
- Outdoor space
- Water container
- Brushes

What to do:

1. Draw a variety of familiar 2D shape outlines in chalk on a concrete or hard surface in an outdoor space.
2. Fill containers with clean water and add brushes.
3. Invite the children to use the brushes and water to paint away the outlines of each shape until they have completely disappeared.

What's in it for the children?

This is an invitation to engage with familiar 2D shapes, focusing on characteristics of outlines. This is a brilliant activity to develop first steps into drawing shapes independently.

Taking it forward

- Make chalks available in the space, inviting the children to draw shape outlines for themselves and peers to erase.
- Replace the water and brushes with pebbles and invite the children to overlay each shape outline with the pebbles rather than erasing them.

Natural object sort

What you need:

- A variety of natural objects, e.g. seashells, pebbles, feathers, twigs, leaves, flowers, seed heads, tree seeds such as acorns, conkers, cones

- A shallow basket or tub

What to do:

1. Gather a selection of natural objects. Aim to include differences in scale, colour, texture and weight as well as obvious differences in shape.

2. Assemble the objects in a shallow basket or tub and place it so that it is easily accessible to a small group of children.

3. Talk with the children about the idea of regular shapes that we give names to.

4. Invite the children to name as many different shapes as they can.

5. After identifying a few regular shape names, turn the children's thinking to irregular shapes. Explain that some shapes, often those we find in nature, aren't exactly the shapes we have already talked about but they are close and can also be sorted into groups based on shape criteria, e.g. round or curvy, pointy, flat, with corners.

6. Offer the basket of natural objects to the children.

7. Ask them to work together to see if they can sort the objects into groups according to shape.

8. Allow the children time to talk and work together, independent of adult support, before returning to check in on progress.

9. Talk with the children about their selected criteria and resulting groups and decisions.

What's in it for the children?

The world of shape is a complex one that the children will investigate and learn more about as they grow but it's certainly a world where many objects can't be described with a regular shape name. This activity aims to allow time to focus on introducing and exploring the idea of irregular shapes using a practical challenge with a tactile, familiar group of objects.

Taking it forward

- Invite the children to bring their own collected natural objects into the setting for this activity.

50 fantastic ideas for exploring shape and pattern

Painting around
3D shape

What you need:

- Selection of different-shaped solid 3D objects, e.g. boxes, cartons, tubes
- Paper
- Paint

What to do:

1. Discuss the 3D objects with the children, identify the shapes by name. Compare the different shapes.

2. Select one object and ask the children to guess what would happen if you were to draw around the object. What shape would they see?

3. Place your chosen object onto a surface and draw around the perimeter with your finger.

4. Discuss and compare children's different ideas and thinking.

5. Place the object onto paper and paint around the outside edges while the children observe.

6. Talk about the shape that you have created as it is revealed. Point out the sides, corners, curves and name the 2D shape.

7. Invite the children to independently repeat the process, selecting and painting around the different objects, revealing the 2D shapes created by their flat different surfaces.

What's in it for the children?

This is a simple and interesting way to introduce or further explore the relationship between 3D and 2D shapes. It is also an opportunity to use shape-related vocabulary such as 'flat', 'curved', 'straight', 'corner', 'edge', 'point' and 'side' in context and, if desired, introduce the term 'face'.

Taking it forward

- Set up a table-top display of the flat painted outlines alongside the solid objects, creating a matching activity.

- Printing with the faces of 3D shapes using paint is a natural progression from this activity.

50 fantastic ideas for exploring shape and pattern

Sculpt
3D shape

What you need:

- Clay
- Water bowl
- Mats
- A set of regular 3D shapes

What to do:

1. Each child will require a good-sized ball of clay, a mat and access to a water bowl.

2. Set up the materials on a working surface along with a set of regular 3D shapes.

3. Invite the children to choose a shape and make a clay model of it.

4. Depending on their experience and confidence, work alongside the children, demonstrating how to roll, squash and shape using fingers and hands. Model how to check your work against your chosen regular 3D shape from the set.

5. Allow plenty of time for independent play.

6. Ideally, leave the resources out for several days so the children can return and revisit with refined ideas, experience and growing awareness of the properties of each shape.

7. Encourage children to share their models with peers and adults; reinforce shape names.

What's in it for the children?

This is a surprisingly challenging task – it appears simple but requires close observation and real focus to shape the clay into a recognisable desired shape. This activity also provides a good opportunity to learn and use the names of the 3D shapes; these are often much less familiar to younger children.

Taking it forward

- To offer challenge to more experienced children, invite them to play a guessing game with a partner. Ask them to create a shape and have their partner correctly identify which shape they were aiming to replicate.

- You may wish to include shaping tools along with the basic materials.

Shape sort challenge
3D shape

What you need:

- 3D shapes, e.g. wooden blocks
- Container
- Timers: one minute, three minutes, five minutes
- Sorting hoops (optional)

What to do:

1. Gather together a quantity of 3D shapes. Wooden blocks in a variety of regular 3D shapes are great for this activity.

2. Set out the shapes, in an accessible container, along with three timers and sorting hoops if desired.

3. Explain to the children that they going to sort the shapes into groups against the timer.

4. Either stipulate which timer each child is going to work with based on assessment knowledge of their experience or allow the children to experiment with the three timers, comparing how many shapes they can successfully sort within each time.

5. Make this activity available for independent use within your provision to allow the children to revisit it.

What's in it for the children?

This is a fun invitation to develop sight recognition and familiarity with 3D shapes. The timers add an additional aspect of engagement and allow children to see progress in their learning as they become more adept at sorting against the clock.

Taking it forward

- Invite the children to race against each other or to work in teams while completing the activity.

- Make and offer photocards with an image of each shape along with its name to be used during the activity.

Print a picture

3D shape

What you need:

- Paint
- Shallow trays
- A4 paper
- Set of small 3D shapes
- Wipes or tissues

Top tip ⭐

It takes young children a little while to become adept at making a clear print, rather than sliding or drawing with the shapes so allow time for this.

What's in it for the children?

This is a creative opportunity to begin to relate 3D and 2D shapes through direct discovery and investigation. As children's knowledge and understanding grows, they will have fun creating printed pictures. This activity also promotes correct use of shape names and an opportunity to introduce the use of 'face' as a shape term.

Taking it forward

- Share this activity with caregivers as something that can be tried at home with packaging destined for the recycling bin.
- Play matching games with 2D and 3D shapes, pairing them up according to surfaces.
- Use the shapes to print a repeating pattern rather than a picture.

What to do:

1. Set up the paint in the shallow trays alongside the paper. Set out the 3D shapes and wipes or tissues so that everything is accessible.

2. Gather the children and explain that they are each going to use the materials to make a picture by printing with the shapes.

3. Demonstrate how to dip each shape into the paint and print with it onto the paper. Verbalise your actions, e.g. 'I'm dipping this cylinder. Look, it's made a different shape when I've printed, the flat surface has made a circle.'

4. Have wipes or tissues close by to ensure the shapes don't become unmanageably saturated in paint.

5. Invite the children to use the materials to investigate shapes they can print and pictures they can create.

6. Allow lots of time for children to return to this activity as their understanding grows with experience; encourage them to share and display their printed pictures.

Sides, edges and corners

3D shape

What you need:

- Salt dough
- Wooden toothpicks
- Sets of 2D and 3D shapes

What to do:

1. Roll the salt dough into medium-sized balls, one per child.

2. Arrange the toothpicks, dough and shapes together in a space where children can work together.

3. Show the children how to connect the toothpicks together using a small ball of dough.

4. Ask a child to choose a shape from the sets and demonstrate how to recreate the outline of the shape using the materials.

5. As you demonstrate, talk about making sides and corners with 2D shapes and edges with 3D. You are not aiming for the children to correctly use these terms, but introducing vocabulary so it is heard and becomes familiar at this stage is important.

6. Compare the final shape with the initial choice from the set.

7. Invite the children to work in pairs to select and build different shapes.

8. Encourage perseverance and create a display space to celebrate completed shapes.

What's in it for the children?

This is an opportunity to use relatively unfamiliar materials to create 3D or 2D shapes. While completing this activity, children will reinforce shape recognition and correct use of shape vocabulary. This is a practical opportunity to use materials to create each shape accurately. Working with others encourages discussion of attributes as the shape is created.

Taking it forward

● Offer a challenge that requires application, e.g. create a home for a character or create a shape for a play park.

✚ Health & Safety

You may wish to supervise the children when working with these materials, depending on their age and stage of development.

Wrap it up
3D shape

What you need:

- Rolls of wrapping paper
- Scissors
- Sticky tape, in a dispenser if available
- Selection of objects, cartons, tubes, boxes in a variety of regular and irregular 3D shapes and sizes

What's in it for the children?

This activity challenges some adults, so it offers plenty of challenge for young children! While wrapping an object, the focus is entirely on the shape of the object – from observing the shape, manipulating the shape while trying to cover and secure with the paper to finally seeing the flat surfaces, curves and sharp corners appear from under the wrapping paper.

Taking it forward

- As a precursor to this activity, create patterned wrapping paper with the children.
- Wrap a selection of 3D shapes and have the children match the wrapped shape to a corresponding set of photographs taken before the object was wrapped.

What to do:

1. This wrapping activity could stand alone as an activity during a shape focus within your setting. You could also link this opportunity to a moment of celebration such as a birthday or to a seasonal festival.

2. Set up the materials as accessibly as possible to allow for independent use. Pre-cut the wrapping paper into sheets.

3. Model how to wrap an object with the paper and tape while the children observe.

4. Invite the children to work independently or with others to wrap the objects.

5. Link this wrapping opportunity to a story. Set the context of choosing and wrapping presents for a specific character or event, such as a birthday present or house move, within a story.

The shape of things
Shape in the wider world

What you need:

- Access to a digital camera and a computer for showing the images or printing out
- Regular 2D and 3D shapes for reinforcement and recognition

Top tip

Limiting the conversation exclusively to shape may feel unnatural and the children may quickly lose interest. Try to find a balance between focusing the children's thinking while still allowing space to share their individual thoughts and ideas.

What's in it for the children?

This activity provides an opportunity to bring shape awareness and recognition into the familiar context of the children's local environment. Discussion of the images should prompt thinking and observation beyond the setting. Sharing this activity with caregivers can further reinforce recognition and awareness when the children are out and about in the locality.

Taking it forward

- Provide drawing materials and invite the children to replicate one of the photos, attempting to correctly represent the shapes in their drawing.
- Take the children out into the local area to capture their own images.
- Share this activity with caregivers, encouraging them to look around and talk about the shapes that they can see as they travel to and from the setting.

What to do:

1. Spend time in the local area with your camera taking images of objects, places, buildings, signs: anything striking, interesting or thought provoking that will stimulate interest and discussion with the children. Try to include landmarks and places familiar to all as well as the more unusual.

2. Print and laminate the images to create a set of photocards or edit ready to share electronically.

3. Share the images with the children.

4. Lead the discussion explaining that you would like them to think carefully about the shape of things around your setting.

5. Questions or prompts may include:

   - What shapes do you notice around you when you are on your way here?

   - What shapes are the buildings you see?

   - What about other things? What shape are they?

   - Let's look at this picture, what can you tell me about it?

   - I can see different shapes in this picture, can we name any?

   - I can see different shapes in this picture, can we describe them?

   - There are lots of different shapes here, I wonder how many we can spot?

   - Look, there's a triangular-shaped roof. Are all roofs triangular shaped?

   - How many windows can we see? Are they all the same shape?

   - I wonder why that is a ... shape?

Self-portraits

Shape in the wider world

What you need:

- A4 paper in skin tones
- Scissors
- Laminator
- Hand-held mirrors
- Whiteboard
- Coloured dough
- Camera

What's in it for the children?

This is an opportunity to look closely at one of the shapes we perhaps observe the most in everyday life – our face and the faces of those around us. Although our individual features make us who we are, all faces have the same basic shapes. Observation and discussion during this activity promotes the use of appropriate shape-related descriptive language such as 'round', 'curved', 'long', 'pointy', 'short', 'side', 'outside', 'circle' and 'oval'.

Taking it forward

- Work entirely in dough, creating a 3D head with features.
- Pair the children and invite them to use the materials to shape a portrait of their partner.
- Provide drawing materials and mirrors and ask the children to draw a self-portrait.

What to do:

1. Cut the paper into face shapes and laminate them. These will be used as mats.
2. Present the mirrors to the children, one per child works best.
3. Ask the children to look carefully into the mirror at their face and to describe the different shapes they can see.
4. Draw a large face shape on the whiteboard. As the children observe and describe facial shapes, draw in and refine the features as they name them.
5. Following this focused observation and discussion, give each child a laminated face shape, ensuring they have access to the dough.
6. Invite the children to create a representation of their face on the mat using dough. Encourage them to pay close attention to each feature and its shape, continuing to check and use the mirror as they work.
7. Encourage the children to share, compare and discuss their portraits as they work.
8. Take a photograph of each completed portrait before it is deconstructed.

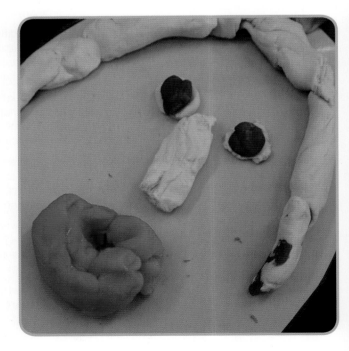

What shape is my body?

Shape in the wider world

What you need:

- Rolls of lining paper
- Sticky tape
- Paint and brushes or chunky washable fibre-tip pens
- Wipes
- Camera

Top tip ⭐

When creating a display of the completed outlines, allow the children to cut around the bodies, giving them a greater experience of shape and scale.

What's in it for the children?

This is an exciting, practical opportunity to think about and investigate shape on a large scale. It's a superb context to discuss the idea of a whole shape being made up of a several different individual shapes.

Taking it forward

- Allow the children to use paint to turn the giant body outlines into life-size self-portraits.

- Link to an enquiry on the human body by asking the children to draw or paint onto their giant outline what they think is inside their body.

- Link to literacy by encouraging the children to choose a story character and use paint to turn their giant outline into their chosen character.

What to do:

1. This activity works best in pairs or very small groups. Gather the children together and explain that you would like them to think about the shape of their bodies.

2. Ask, 'What shapes are our bodies? Are they one big shape or lots of different shapes?'

3. Spend time sharing the children's ideas, noting down their thoughts and explanations; allow them to use their whole bodies to show their thinking.

4. Explain to the children that they are going to work together to make pictures showing the shapes of their bodies.

5. Work with the children to roll out and secure the paper onto the floor with tape.

6. Explain to the children that they are going to choose one person to lay down on the paper while the group draws or paints around them.

7. Discuss safety and trust. Agree together that there should be no fingers or bodies stepped on and no clothes or bodies with paint or pen on at the end of the session – unless it's a real accident.

8. Keep wipes close by to wipe off any paint or pen if it accidentally makes contact with skin or clothing.

9. Allow lots of time for the children to work together to produce their giant body outlines. Photograph the children at work.

10. Encourage the children to talk about the finished outlines, comparing these to their original ideas. Prompt them to use the language of shape to describe and compare.

11. Create a display of these outlines along with the notes from discussion and images of the activity being completed.

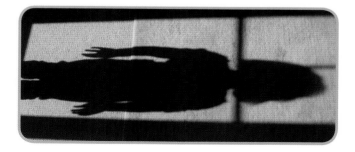

Spider's web

Shape in the wider world

What you need:

- Photographs of spiders' webs
- Outdoor space (optional)
- Whiteboards and pens
- Geoboards
- Elastic bands
- Online access via an interactive whiteboard or tablet

What to do:

1. Talk together about spider webs with the children. Ask, 'I wonder how a spider weaves each web?'

2. Look closely and discuss the photographs of webs. If possible, take a focused walk into an outdoor environment to look for webs.

3. Ask lots of wondering questions to generate interest, e.g. 'I wonder what they're made from?' and 'I wonder where we'd find the most webs?'

4. After looking at and discussing real webs and photographs, focus the children's thinking on shape.

5. Ask the children, 'Are they all the same shape? What different shapes can we see?'

6. Invite the children to work in small groups and use a whiteboard to draw a picture of a web, thinking carefully about the overall shape and the pattern inside the web.

7. Invite the children to share their drawings with the group and explain the shape(s) they have drawn.

8. Provide each small group with a geoboard and bands.

9. Invite the group to make a web on the geoboard, using their drawing as a plan.

10. After each group has completed their web, gather the children together and watch an online clip of a spider creating a web.

11. Ask the groups to begin making a new web, this time thinking about recreating the shapes they watched the spider create and the order in which they were created.

12. Share results with the group.

13. Round off the experience by showing and sharing 2D multi-sided shapes perhaps from beyond the children's experience, e.g. pentagons, hexagons, octagons, nonagons, decagons.

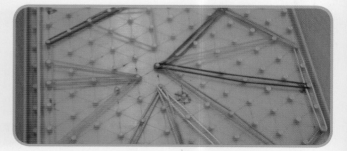

What's in it for the children?

This provides a practical opportunity to discover more about the shape of a familiar object. The context of a spider's web is a great introduction to moving beyond the basic 2D shapes that children may be familiar with, introducing the idea that there are five-, six-, seven-, eight- and nine-sided shapes and beyond! Working together creates real opportunity for discussion and the use of shape-related language in context.

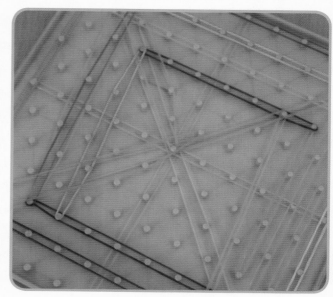

Taking it forward

- Investigate the shape of other animals' homes, e.g. cone-shaped birds' nests and hexagonal honey bee combs are both interesting shapes to explore.

Buildings of the world

Shape in the wider world

What you need:

- Photographs of famous buildings from around the world, e.g. the Eiffel Tower, the Shard, the Taj Mahal, Buckingham Palace, the Colosseum, Sydney Opera House, Saint Basil's Cathedral, the Leaning Tower of Pisa, the Louvre Museum, the Giza Pyramids and the Space Needle
- Backing card
- Building blocks, including cubes, cuboids, cylinders, triangular prisms, square-based pyramids
- Camera

What's in it for the children?

Introducing the children to a range of famous buildings broadens their awareness of shape in the wider world. This activity aims to encourage careful observation of 3D shapes while challenging the children to match, select and build rather than simply to name or describe. While building, children are comparing and selecting based on what's available as well as what's required and, in doing so, they are thinking carefully about similarities and differences between shapes.

Taking it forward

- Focus on one building. Make available a different modelling material such as clay and encourage the children to recreate the building using this material.
- Challenge the children to design and build the next world-famous building. Ask them to think about its use and to give it a name.

What to do:

1. Create a set of photocards of famous buildings from around the world using photographs found online and sturdy backing card.

2. Display the images around or within an area where the children have space to build using the blocks.

3. Draw the children's attention to the images. Discuss the buildings, encouraging the children to share their observations before sharing their names, locations, materials used to build and so on. Discussion does not need to include naming shapes. The aim of the discussion is to generate interest and motivation.

4. Challenge the children to use the blocks to make any of the buildings.

5. Allow time for independent and shared building attempts.

6. Plan to work alongside the children. During this time, you may verbalise their actions or guess at their thinking, e.g. 'I can see you've used a lot of this shape. Do you know what it is? That tower has seven cylinders and they are all balanced.' Keep the focus on maintaining interest, encouraging observation and interaction with the shapes and not on naming them.

7. Take photographs of building attempts and allow the children to take photographs of completed models to allow the materials to be reused.

8. Display your photographs alongside the photocards of the original buildings.

> **Top tip** ⭐
>
> Ensure that the building blocks provided are going to be able to create semi-recognisable if not recognisable models of the buildings.

Fruit and vegetable prints

Shape in the wider world

What you need:

- Fruit and vegetables
- A sharp knife
- Shallow trays
- Paint
- Paper

What's in it for the children?

This is an opportunity to use familiar objects to think about and explore different shapes. Discussion after the activity encourages use of shape-related language, e.g. 'curved', 'flat', 'corner', 'side', to describe attributes as well as language related to everyday irregular shapes, e.g. 'jagged' and 'smooth'. Children can be encouraged to use comparative language too, e.g. 'It's like a flower shape.' Printing with a 3D solid shape to create a 2D flat image highlights the connection and distinction between the two.

Taking it forward

- Try potato printing with the children. Cut potatoes in half and use a knife to create a stamp on the cross section as a fun supplementary activity.

- Revisit this activity in different seasons exploring the selection of fruit and vegetables available at the time.

- Use the same fruit and vegetables and child-safe knives; allow the children to cut shapes into different sections.

What to do:

1. Cut the fruit and vegetables into sections. Aim for differing cross-section shapes and scales but ensure that the children will find it manageable to handle, dip and print with the stamps you create.

2. Present the fruit and vegetable shapes in a shallow tray, alongside paint in shallow trays and paper to print onto.

3. Invite the children to independently use the fruit and vegetable stamps to create prints.

4. Ask them to look closely as they explore, thinking about the shapes that they can see both on the food itself and what is being printed on the paper.

5. Follow up with a group discussion talking about different shapes and any other observations the children have about the experience. Refer back to the fruit and vegetable stamps as well as the prints during discussion. Emphasise appropriate use of shape-related language.

Cloud spotting

Shape in the wider world

What you need:

- Whiteboard
- Photographs of clouds
- Outdoor space or an unobstructed view of the sky
- Blue paper
- White paint
- Paintbrushes

What's in it for the children?

This activity encourages the children to look at and discuss shapes within their everyday world. Through discussion, children are hearing and using shape names and shape-related language.

Taking it forward

- In an outdoor space, place a child-safe mirror on a flat surface or directly on the ground along with whiteboard pens. Invite the children to capture the shapes of the clouds by drawing around them on the mirror.

- Provide equipment for the children to photograph cloudy skies and display these on an interactive whiteboard once back indoors. Discuss the shapes and pictures that can be seen.

What to do:

1. Introduce this activity by sharing a scenario with the children. Explain that as you left home and looked up at the sky, you saw the most amazing straight line stretching across as far as you could see and then you saw a cloud in the shape of a dragon. Ask the children if they have ever seen lines or cloud shapes that looked like objects or pictures in the sky.

2. Allow children time to discuss and share their experiences; some of these may be very imaginative!

3. Add to the discussion by using a whiteboard to draw the shapes being discussed. Encourage the children to use the whiteboard independently to draw as they share.

4. Source and share photographs of clouds forming different familiar shapes. There are many available online.

5. Try to leave interpretation of the photographs as open ended as possible.

6. Ask the children what you might see if you looked up at the sky right now.

7. Head outdoors or use a window with a clear view of the sky. What can they see?

8. Provide blue paper and white paint and invite the children to paint their own cloud formations. What different clouds can they come up with? What shapes will they choose?

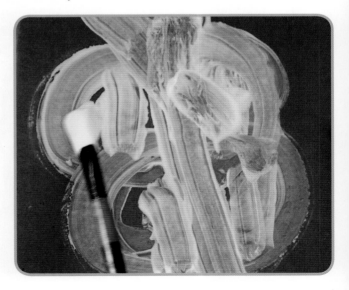

Mirror play

Shape in the wider world

What you need:

- Selection of child-friendly portable and hand-held mirrors
- Camera

What's in it for the children?

This is a fun, engaging and open-ended context to begin to introduce and use the language of reflection. Investigating reflections involves exploring the characteristics of shapes and objects from another angle.

Taking it forward

- Lead a focused talking and thinking discussion on where we use and require mirrors in everyday life.
- Include mirrors as part of everyday provision within the learning environment once the focus has passed.

What to do:

1. Create an accessible table-top interactive display as an invitation for children to explore a selection of child-friendly mirrors.

2. Encourage the children to play and explore with the mirrors throughout the indoor and outdoor environment.

3. Allow time for the children to make discoveries and follow lines of exploration independent of adult intervention.

4. Generate interest in the mirrors by observing and noting the children's discoveries, highlighting and sharing their thinking and learning with the wider group.

5. If necessary, ask 'What happens if…?', 'What do you see…?', 'Have you tried…?' and 'I wonder…?' type questions to prompt thinking and investigation.

6. Take photographs of the children exploring the mirrors and display these alongside the mirrors.

Loose parts
Repeating and symmetrical pattern

What you need:

- Variety of loose parts in groups or multiples
- Shallow baskets or trays with dividers

What to do:

1. Present the loose parts in shallow baskets or trays.
2. To ensure the focus remains on pattern making, it may be best to model this activity.
3. Begin by selecting objects and placing them, one after another, in a horizontal line. Talk aloud, explaining your process as you work: 'I'm going to choose this and put it here, then I'm going to choose this one. I'll need another one of these, then I'll need…'
4. Once a simple linear repeating pattern has been made, begin at one end and work through to the other, pointing to each part of the pattern in turn, verbalising and emphasising the repetition while the children observe.
5. Challenge the children to use the materials to create their own repeating patterns.
6. Allow time for collaboration and discussion; patterns do not have to be created independently.
7. Encourage experienced children to become aware of how many different objects are being included in their pattern.
8. Specifically ask children to make a pattern with two different things, three different things and so on.

Top tip ⭐

Reuse and recycle is the key with loose parts. Collect small groups of familiar, interesting, readily sourced materials – aim for wide appeal with a range of colour and themes.

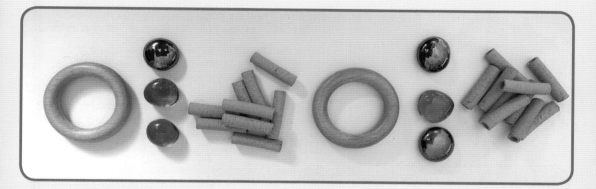

What's in it for the children?

An appealing selection of loose parts helps to ensure that all children become interested in creating a repeating pattern. Often pattern making materials can be rather feminine and the use of loose parts aims to address this. The open-ended nature of loose parts ensures that this is an accessible activity that can be differentiated to make it increasingly simple or complex depending on the experience and understanding of the children.

Taking it forward

- Provide equipment for the children to capture images of these transient patterns. Use the images for discussion, display or as templates for peers to recreate.

Dinosaur footprints

Repeating and symmetrical pattern

What you need:

- Roll or large sheets of plain paper
- Model dinosaur toys – any size
- Basket
- Storybook
- Coloured paints

Top tip ⭐

If dinosaurs aren't available, other animals also work well.

What to do:

1. Place the paper on a flat, easily accessible surface.
2. Gather the dinosaurs together into an accessible basket or container.
3. Working with a group of children, begin by sharing a story with a dinosaur theme or by exploring stomping, romping dinosaur movements together within an open space.
4. Explain that during this activity, the children are going to use the dinosaurs to make patterns on the paper as they stomp with paint-covered feet.
5. Drop lines and circles of paint directly onto the surface of the paper for the children to dip the dinosaurs into.
6. Allow the children time to use the dinosaurs and paint to create different patterns either independently or collaboratively. The children could create patterns through the direction and placement of the footprints or by repeating colour selection and placement. You may wish to direct their focus or leave this activity open ended, depending on the stage and experience of the children.
7. Take time to return to the dinosaur prints once dry to discuss and identify any patterns that have been created.
8. You may wish to allow ongoing access to this experience for a period to enable the children to explore, develop and refine their ideas.

What's in it for the children?

This is a fun, large-scale context to explore patterns created by moving an object through paint or by repeat printing in different directions or with changing colours.

Taking it forward

- Allowing the children to create their own footprint patterns with paint on large rolls of paper is a fun complimentary experience to this activity.
- Limit the colour choice to two colours only and challenge the children to produce two patterns each.

Bunting

Repeating and symmetrical pattern

What you need:

- Sturdy card
- Scissors
- Variety of patterned fabrics and/or patterned papers
- Twine
- Pegs
- Basket

What's in it for the children?

This is a practical opportunity to create repeating patterns that can be modified easily, worked on individually or with peers and which can be differentiated using the same materials.

Taking it forward

- Provide drawing materials to give children the opportunity to record their patterns.

- Lead a group activity creating patterns that have obvious errors in the repeat. Ask the children to use the bunting to correct them.

- For a simpler experience, provide single-coloured triangles rather than including patterns.

What to do:

1. Cut a triangular bunting card template around 5 cm in length along the shortest side.

2. Use the template as a guide to cut triangles out of the different patterned pieces of card and fabric. You will require multiples of each.

3. Secure a washing line, using the twine, at child height for the bunting triangles to be pinned onto. It's vital to choose a safe space within your setting.

4. Set out the pegs and bunting triangles in a basket beside the washing line.

5. Use the triangles to create a repeating bunting pattern ready for the children to discover and discuss on arrival.

6. Ask the children to create new patterns using the materials.

Top tip

Avoid choosing patterns that are overtly 'feminine'. Think about including camouflage, black and white or animal print. Wrapping paper can be a brilliant source of patterns for all interests.

Towers
Repeating and symmetrical pattern

What you need:

- Wide straws in a variety of colours
- Scissors
- Basket
- Glue gun
- Used jar lids
- Wooden skewers or round lolly sticks

What's in it for the children?

You may choose to take this opportunity to introduce and demonstrate the concept of repeating pattern. Alternatively, you can use this activity to consolidate their existing knowledge and allow them to spend time using the materials to create simple repeating colour patterns.

Taking it forward

- To simplify this activity, create a repeating pattern on one skewer and ask the children to copy it on another.

- Place drawing materials alongside, encouraging the children to record their patterns. Squared paper adds interest.

- Replace the skewers with dry spaghetti strands pushed into play dough to add an additional challenging element of fine motor work to this experience.

What to do:

1. Cut the wide straws into smaller lengths approximately 2 cm each. Put the pieces in a basket.

2. Place a blob of glue on the centre of the jar lid and hold a skewer in place to stabilise until the glue has set and the skewer is held securely in place.

3. Set up the skewers on a flat surface and place the straw pieces within easy reach.

4. Invite the children to stack the straws onto the skewers. Allow time for open exploration at first.

5. Ask the children to use the materials to create a repeating pattern.

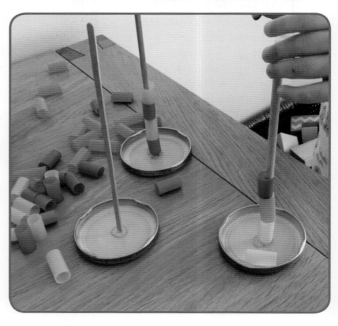

Pairs

Repeating and symmetrical pattern

What you need:

- Plain card
- Scissors
- Wrapping or patterned paper
- Glue

Top tip

Ensure card is thick enough for the patterns not to show through the back of the playing cards.

What's in it for the children?

This is an opportunity to explore and describe different patterns. The game of pairs provides a play context for children to visually discriminate between different patterns.

Taking it forward

- To make the game more challenging, restrict the patterns to a single colour ensuring that the children focus entirely on differences in shape, position and line.

What to do:

1. Cut blank card into rectangles approximately 5 cm by 4 cm – these will become the playing cards. Each child will require at least two cards and the minimum required for a game would be eight cards.

2. Present the blanks cards and patterned paper to the children. Explain that they are going to create their own cards to play a game of pattern pairs.

3. Model the next part of the activity for the children. Select a piece of patterned paper. Cut or tear it so that it is the same size or smaller than your blank playing card. Glue the patterned paper to your playing card and repeat this process for another card, using the same patterned paper to create a matching pair.

4. Give two blank cards to each child and invite them to use the patterned paper to make two matching playing cards for a game.

5. Take time to look at and discuss the patterns on all of the completed cards. Ensure that each card has a match and remake cards together if necessary.

6. Pool the cards together face down in the centre of the table.

7. The children take it in turns to select and turn over two cards. If the cards match, they keep them. If not, they are returned to the table.

8. Play until all cards are taken. The winner has the highest number of pairs.

Number patterns

Repeating and symmetrical pattern

What you need:

- Cards, blocks or other materials showing digits 0–9 (you will need multiples of each)

Top tip ⭐

Less-experienced children naturally enjoy sequencing digits from 0–9 if this is recently acquired knowledge. If this happens, reduce the digit choice to three digits to maintain the focus on pattern making.

What to do:

1. This activity works best if introduced and supported by an adult initially.

2. Explain to the children that you are going to make a pattern with the numbers.

3. Choose and arrange some numbers into a repeating pattern; begin with a very simple two-digit repeat, e.g. 3, 4, 3, 4, 3, 4.

4. Invite the children to verbalise the pattern along with you as you point to each number in the sequence.

5. Challenge them to continue the pattern both verbally and with the digits.

6. Repeat the final step of verbalising the pattern together. Explain that this is an excellent strategy for 'checking' the correctness of a pattern.

7. Invite the children to work independently to create repeating number patterns.

What's in it for the children?

This is a practical activity that introduces simple repeating number patterns.

Taking it forward

- As a warm up activity, chant verbal number patterns together.

- Provide writing materials and encourage children to record their pattern.

- As a next step, have the children work in pairs. The leader makes a pattern and the partner copies.

Penguin parade
Repeating and symmetrical pattern

What you need:

- Interactive whiteboard or tablet with internet access
- Penguin templates
- Coloured fibre-tip pens, crayons or paints

What's in it for the children?

This activity focuses on describing, naming and recreating common design patterns. Children will be familiar with some of these patterns from clothing and decoration. This works well as either an introduction to different pattern designs or as a culmination of a focus.

Taking it forward

- Work together to sort the completed penguins into groups of similar patterns.
- Provide children with the opportunity to create many different patterns before selecting one to recreate on their penguin.
- Link to fictional stories of patterned animals such as Elmer the Patchwork Elephant.
- Create a patterned piece of clothing for a favourite fictional character.

What to do:

1. Introduce the idea of a penguin parade to the children by watching and discussing some videos of penguins. An online search for 'penguin parade' will bring up many examples that can be safely shared.

2. Explain to the children that you are going to have a 'patterned penguin parade' within your setting where they are each going to create their own patterned penguin to join the parade.

3. Ask, 'What type of pattern could you have on your penguin?' Discuss and share all ideas, generating enthusiasm at this stage.

4. Depending on experience, ideas may include spotty, dotty, stripy, checked, scrolling, loopy, swirling, camouflage, diagonal lines, floral, geometric or tartan.

5. Look at examples of these suggestions together online, or provide paper and fabric samples.

6. Create a simple penguin shape template with one piece of card and use this to produce enough blank penguins for at least one per child. Approximately 12 cm in height works well but change this to suit your children's needs and the materials available.

7. Invite the children to create their patterned penguin ready for the parade.

8. Depending on space and time, there are a several parade options: the finished patterned penguins could be used to create a wall display at child height; the children could walk with their penguins recreating their very own parade; or the finished penguins could be attached to card tubes and displayed on a table top creating an interactive display that becomes an activity in itself.

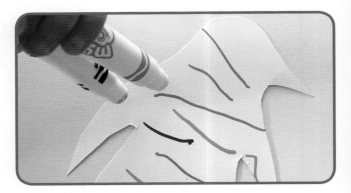

Patchwork picnic

Repeating and symmetrical pattern

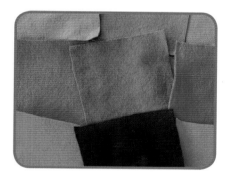

Top tip

Take a photograph of the layout before disassembling to make it easier to sew together.

What's in it for the children?

This is a practical experience which allows the children the opportunity to think about and find out how coloured patterns are created and how different choices change the look of a coloured pattern.

Taking it forward

- Create a small-scale patchwork experience using gummed paper and plain paper, inviting the children to create their own patterned patchwork picnic blankets.

What to do:

1. Cut the felt into squares around 8 cm by 8 cm. You will require enough squares to make a play blanket when joined together.

2. Discuss the idea of a picnic with the children. Let them share their experiences and identify items necessary for any picnic. Share a story if experiences are limited and support is necessary.

3. Explain to the children that you have all of the things they need to play picnics with teddies or toys but you don't have a picnic blanket. Set out the teddies, soft toys and the picnic set.

4. Explain that you are going to work together to make a blanket for their play.

5. Bring out the felt square patches and begin to lay them beside each other in long rows, encouraging the children to join in.

6. Work until the felt squares are all laid out together.

7. Stand back and discuss the finished result with the children asking, 'Are we happy with that? Would we like to change anything?'

8. Allow time for the children to move the felt squares around with your support until they are satisfied with the final placement of the squares. Possibilities include striped rows of one colour, squares of one colour, random colour placement, repeating colour patterns, horizontal, vertical and diagonal colour patterns. Depending on your chosen focus and experience of the group, you may wish to think aloud and show some of these possibilities to the children.

9. Having created the final placement together, use sewing materials to join the squares together. A sewing machine is quickest, but hand-sewing works equally well.

10. Introduce the final patchwork picnic blanket to the children and place alongside the teddies, soft toys and picnic set for independent play.

Portrait patterns

Repeating and symmetrical pattern

What you need:

- Camera
- Computer or tablet
- Printer
- Scissors
- Laminator

What's in it for the children?

This is a fun and engaging personalised resource to make and use within your setting aimed at building experience of creating and extending a repeating pattern. Even the most reluctant children will enjoy using photographs of themselves and peers to learn more about this concept.

Taking it forward

- Take and incorporate photos of practitioners and other adults within your setting.

- Share this activity with caregivers as it can be easily recreated with family members.

What to do:

1. Take head and shoulders photos of each child within the group or setting, or invite the children to take photos of each other to involve them in the creation of this resource.

2. Use computer equipment or printing facilities to resize the photos, copy and paste four per A4 page, creating four mini portraits of each child.

3. Print the portraits, cut and laminate to create four portrait cards per child.

4. Present the cards to the group, inviting them to independently use them to create 'people patterns'.

5. Encourage children to use these materials with others, generating discussion and engagement.

Mandalas
Repeating and symmetrical pattern

What you need:

- Coloured card
- Scissors
- Clear sticky-back plastic
- Coloured tissue paper
- Small baskets
- Access to online images of mandala patterns

What's in it for the children?

This is a colourful opportunity to create a repeating pattern 'in the round' and to begin to introduce and develop a sense of reflectional symmetry.

Taking it forward

- Search online for 'nature mandalas' and discuss the inspiring results. Provide plates filled with sand and a variety of natural materials, e.g. shells, pebbles, seeds, flower heads, and invite the children to make their own nature mandalas.

- Replace tissue paper squares with flower petals collected from nature.

- Print off mandala patterns for the children to colour in. There are thousands available copyright free online.

What to do:

1. To make the mandala circle, begin by cutting circles of card 20 cm in diameter. Cut away the interiors to create circular frames 1 cm in width.

2. Cut circles, 20 cm in diameter, from the sticky-back plastic. Peel off and attach the plastic film to the card circles.

3. Cut the tissue paper into squares, 1 cm by 1 cm. Place these in small baskets for the children to access.

4. Show the children photographs of mandalas and discuss the patterns and shapes they can see in them.

5. Demonstrate with a sticky card circle how the children can make a pattern with the coloured squares. Create a simple mandala-style symmetrical pattern on the circle as the children observe.

6. Emphasise that lines are moving around the circle or across the circle from one side to the other, and that colours and sizes are repeated to create the overall pattern.

7. Invite the children to create their own mandala pattern using a sticky card circle and the coloured squares.

8. Edit patterns with the children if appropriate; the materials allow for some movement and repositioning once the squares have been placed. Encourage the children to look at the overall pattern and adjust as necessary.

9. Create a display of the completed patterns.

DIY stampers

Repeating and symmetrical pattern

What you need:

- Very thick cardboard
- Scissors
- Strong sticky tape
- Loose parts, e.g. rubber bands, beads, pom-poms, bottle tops, buttons, straws, bolts
- Strong glue or a glue gun
- Poster paint
- Shallow trays
- Paper

Top tip ⭐

Time spent creating sturdy stampers will pay off in the long run.

What to do:

1. Cut the cardboard into rectangular strips approximately 18 cm by 5 cm. These will become the stampers.

2. Fold or bend the strips into three equal parts, folding each of the ends inwards towards the centre to create a triangular shape.

3. Use sticky tape to secure the ends in place forming a rigid triangular shape with a flat surface that can be held and pressed downwards.

4. Select the loose parts in turn and use strong glue to attach them to the flat surface on each side of the cardboard stamper. Think carefully about the placement of the objects being attached as, once dipped in paint, these will create the pattern being stamped.

5. Allow the stampers to completely dry before use (overnight works best).

6. Gather the stampers together and pour poster paint into shallow trays for dipping; you may wish to limit choice to one colour initially to ensure the focus of pattern remains on the image being stamped.

7. Demonstrate how to hold the rectangular stampers: dip carefully into the paint and apply pressure onto the paper to create a stamped image. Repeat several times side by side or in a horizontal, diagonal or vertical direction to create a simple repeating pattern.

8. Invite the children to create their own patterns.

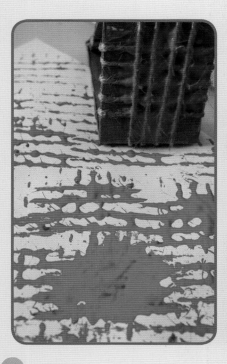

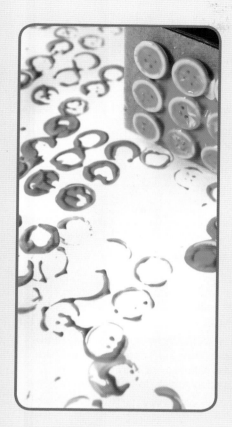

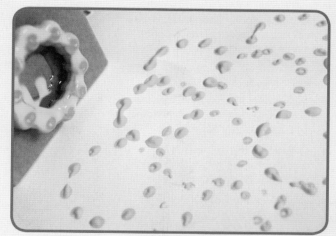

What's in it for the children?

This is an interesting, practical opportunity to make a repeating pattern incorporating shape, position and direction. Using simple materials, children can create patterns ranging from the simplest single image to a complex repeating pattern.

Taking it forward

- Display the different patterns as they are created. Allow time for the children to discuss their process and thinking.

- Expand the paint colour choices.

- Provide salt dough and rolling pins alongside clean stampers. Invite the children to create an imprinted pattern on the surface of the dough.

Autumn leaves
Repeating and symmetrical pattern

What you need:

- A selection of leaves in different shapes and colours
- Shallow basket
- Brown paper, e.g. recycled packaging paper
- Scissors
- PVA glue and brushes

What's in it for the children?

This is an opportunity to use superbly tactile natural material to independently create a simple pattern using shape, colour and size. It is also a great activity to offer over a period of time as materials are relatively free and engaging.

Taking it forward

- Take time outdoors to collect the leaves together with the children as a preparatory activity.

- Investigate the patterns and shapes created with wax crayon leaf rubbings onto paper.

- Create natural leaf pattern crowns by securing the ends of the card to form a crown once the leaves have been stuck on to create a pattern.

What to do:

1. Use the abundance of autumn leaves collected on journeys from home, gathered on outings or within the outdoor space in the setting itself.

2. Create a collection point for the leaves as they arrive.

3. Sift out the strongest colours and most intact leaf shapes for this activity.

4. Present the leaves in a shallow basket.

5. Cut strips of brown paper into lengths approximately 1 m long and 10 cm wide.

6. Place PVA glue and brushes alongside the leaves and paper strips in an accessible area of the provision.

7. Ask the children to use the materials to make a pattern.

8. You may wish to create an example of a simple repeating pattern to show and discuss. If doing so, completely cover each leaf in glue to ensure the leaves last for several days.

9. Invite the children to take these patterns away at the end of each session. This is a super activity to share with caregivers as materials are easy to find in most locations and it's a fun activity to try together at home.

Top tip ⭐

If displaying patterns, ensure the leaves are completely covered in PVA glue to preserve them from quickly drying out in an indoor environment.

Snakes

Repeating and symmetrical pattern

What you need:

- Plain black paper
- Scissors
- Shallow trays
- Bright paint
- Cylindrical objects for stamping, e.g. corks

What to do:

1. Cut black paper into strips approximately 20 cm by 4 cm. Trim curves around the outside to create a snake shape.
2. Fill shallow trays with different coloured bright paints.
3. Set up the paper, paint and stampers together, ready for independent access.
4. Invite the children to use the materials to make a repeating pattern on the snakes.
5. Create examples of patterns while the children observe if necessary.

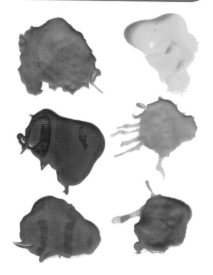

What's in it for the children?

This is an engaging opportunity to create a repeating pattern. Children can successfully access this activity at different levels, making it as simple or as complex as required.

Taking it forward

- To give this activity more focus, reduce the colour choice to two colours and use these to demonstrate a number of different repeating patterns. Challenge the children to see how many permutations they can discover.

- Replace coloured paints with glue and coloured pom-poms or buttons.

Pattern matching blocks

Repeating and symmetrical pattern

What you need:

- Wooden construction blocks
- Fabric in a variety of patterns
- Scissors
- Strong glue

What to do:

1. Select two blocks.
2. Cut a piece of fabric the exact shape and size as one face on each block. Drawing around the block is the quickest method.
3. Glue the fabric to each of the blocks, on one face only.
4. Repeat until you have created a set of pattern blocks with at least two blocks for each pattern represented.
5. Invite the children to play with and explore the pattern blocks.
6. Encourage the children to select and match similar patterns.
7. Discuss contrasts between the patterns as the children explore.
8. Play a game of pairs with the blocks.

What's in it for the children?

The wooden blocks when covered with fabric are tactile and inviting. They lend themselves to open-ended investigation but give the authentic opportunity for language development during play. Games or discussions while the children explore the blocks aim to develop observation, descriptive language and simple pattern recognition.

Taking it forward

- Provide blank wooden blocks and resources such as marker pens. Allow the children to create their own matching pattern pairs.
- To give a greater challenge, create a set of blocks with the same colour fabric and very similar patterns, challenging the children's observational skills further.

Finger prints
Repeating and symmetrical pattern

What you need:
- Paint palettes
- Paints
- Small picture frames
- Hand wipes

What to do:
1. Set up small paint palettes with a limited colour palette. For the simplest pattern, this activity will require two colours.

2. Give each child a picture frame and ensure they have access to a paint palette. You may wish to have hand wipes close by.

3. Explain to the children that they are each going to make a patterned picture frame.

4. Demonstrate how to use the paint to create a repeating colour pattern with fingerprints all the way around the frame.

5. Leave the demonstration frame in the area as a visual reminder of the task and, for less-experienced children, as a visual prompt for pattern making.

6. Invite each child to create a patterned frame independently or with adult support depending on requirements.

Top tip ⭐
Make these with a card frame as a first experience and revisit in the context of a special time of year to create gifts for caregivers or as frames for a class portrait gallery.

What's in it for the children?
This is a purposeful opportunity to copy or create and continue a simple repeating pattern.

Taking it forward
- To simplify this experience, create a pattern that the children can copy onto a frame.

DIY scrapers
Repeating and symmetrical pattern

What you need:

- Marker pen
- Large circular object
- Sturdy cardboard
- Scissors
- Ruler
- Craft knife
- Paint
- Shallow trays
- Paper

What to do:

1. Draw around a large circular object roughly 9 cm in diameter directly onto cardboard. Each circle will become two scrapers.

2. Draw and cut a line along the diameter of the circle to create two semi-circular scrapers.

3. The straight edge of each semi-circle will be used to pull the paint across a surface. Cut shapes from the straight edge at different intervals, in different shapes, e.g. bumps, squares and zig zags.

4. Draw a smaller semi-circular shape inside the circular top of the scraper and cut this out using a ruler and a craft knife to create a handle.

5. Set up paint in shallow trays with paper and the scrapers. Alternatively, apply lines of paint directly to the surface of the paper, ready for the scrapers to be pulled through.

6. Invite the children to dip the scrapers into the paint and use them to create and explore patterns and marks across the surface of the paper.

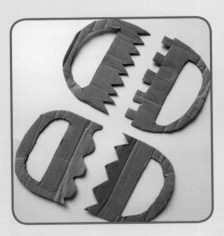

What's in it for the children?

This is an engaging, accessible way to investigate surface pattern making, offering different possibilities and outcomes depending on the way the scrapers are used. It is an activity to return to as children develop in skill and knowledge and have more exposure to pattern as a concept.

Taking it forward

- Set up a continuous length of paper from a roll as an alternative to sheets of paper and invite the children to work collaboratively.

Dice patterns

Repeating and symmetrical pattern

What you need:

- Coloured blocks
- Dice with coloured sides
- White card
- Scissors

What's in it for the children?

This is an opportunity to work with a simple material to make and continue a repeating coloured pattern, made more engaging with the addition of a dice.

Taking it forward

- Adding to the number of colours increases the complexity of this activity.
- Provide paper and coloured pencils to record patterns.
- Replace cubes with squares of gummed paper.

What to do:

1. Set out the coloured blocks ready for use. You will need a die with coloured sides; the colours should correspond to the blocks you have chosen.

2. Cut card into strips, approximately 20 cm long and 5 cm wide. These will be used as base cards for laying patterns.

3. Explain to the children that they are going to work by themselves to roll the dice twice to select their colours before making and continuing a repeating pattern with those colours along the card strip.

4. If they roll the same colour twice, they should re-roll.

5. Support the children as they become familiar with the activity.

6. Encourage them to point to each colour and verbalise the pattern as they make it. This will help them to self-correct any misplaced cubes.

Woolly worms

Repeating and symmetrical pattern

What you need:

- Sturdy plain cardboard
- Scissors
- Googly eyes
- Yarn – two different colours
- Sticky tape

What to do:

1. Cut the cardboard into a worm shape. First cut a rectangle approximately 12 cm by 2 cm. Shape a curved head on one end and leave the other end straight. Each child will require one worm.

2. Attach a googly eye to the curved head.

3. Cut the yarn into lengths of approximately 20 cm.

4. Secure the two lengths of yarn with sticky tape to the end of the worm.

5. You may wish to introduce this activity by discussing worms, sharing children's knowledge of their shape, size, characteristics and experiences of them.

6. Explain to the children that these worms will only be complete when they have a pattern along their body. Ask if anyone can describe the pattern on a worm? Have any of the children seen the stripes on a real worm?

7. While the children observe, show how to wind the wool around the length of the card worm, repeating again and overlaying with the second colour of wool to create stripes.

8. Invite the children to wind their own woolly worms.

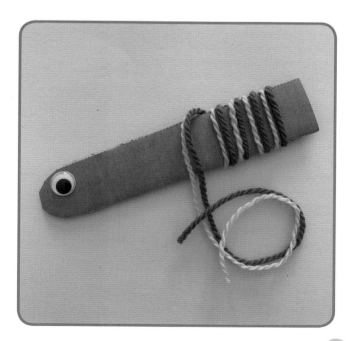

What's in it for the children?

This is an opportunity to use a familiar creature to focus on what a striped pattern looks like before creating and extending a striped pattern of their own.

Taking it forward

- Encourage the children to spot other striped patterns around the setting and share them with the group.

- Provide rulers and drawing materials and invite the children to create more striped patterns.

Finger patterns
Repeating and symmetrical pattern

What you need:

- Sealable food bags
- Paint
- Sticky tape
- Plain card
- Scissors
- Marker pen

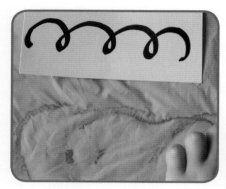

Top tip ⭐

Taping the bags down to the table with sticky tape before use makes them much easier to handle and less prone to alternative investigation.

What's in it for the children?

This experience provides a non-permanent surface to explore copying and continuing a repeating pattern.

Taking it forward

- Offer other non-permanent surfaces for use with the pattern cards, e.g. wet sand, mud, whiteboards, chalkboards.

- Challenge the children to work in pairs. One child can begin the pattern; a friend can continue it.

What to do:

1. Prepare several bags by filling each bag with paint and sealing them with tape. Ensure that the seal is tight and there are no leaks. Do not overfill the bags.

2. Cut the plain card into strips, approximately 7 cm by 3 cm.

3. Draw a different pattern onto each strip with a marker pen. Aim to create a variety of patterns.

4. Set out the activity, one bag per child, which will be used as a drawing surface. Ensure access to the pattern cards.

5. Model the activity for the children. Show them first how to trace along the pattern card with an index finger and then how to copy the same pattern by drawing onto the surface of the paint-filled bag.

6. Invite the children to select one card at a time, copying and continuing the different patterns independently.

Where am I?

Pattern in the wider world

What you need:

- Camera
- Printer

What's in it for the children?

This activity is designed to encourage children to observe, describe and discuss pattern found in their immediate environment. It is also intended to encourage and stimulate pattern awareness beyond the activity.

Taking it forward

- Follow this activity with a pattern hunt in the setting. Give children access to a camera and encourage them to record the patterns that they find.

- Provide drawing materials for the children to replicate the patterns.

What to do:

1. Take a selection of close-up images of patterns within your setting, both indoors and outdoors, in the local area and any other location that you visit. Find examples of interesting patterns that will stimulate discussion, description and thinking.

2. To accompany the pattern photographs, you require a corresponding set of location shots. This may only require a few shots, e.g. the setting indoors, the outdoor area, local park, library. In total there may be fewer location images than pattern images.

3. Print the photographs, creating two sets: pattern and location.

4. Invite the children to work together, independently or with adult support, to sort the patterns into their location.

5. Throughout the activity, encourage the children to describe what they can see, to think about whether they have seen this pattern or something similar and to ask the question 'Where is this?'

Animal patterns

Pattern in the wider world

What you need:

- Tissue paper in a variety of animal prints and patterns
- Shallow containers
- PVA glue in small bowls
- Brushes
- Cardboard tubes
- Images or models of animals with distinctive prints or patterns
- Googly eyes
- Scraps of card, tape and scissors
- Plain paper and drawing pencils

Top tip

Amazing images can be sourced online including moth wings, cheetah fur, elephant skin, snake/fish scales, jaguar coat, bird feathers, giraffe spots and zebra stripes.

What to do:

1. Tear tissue paper into small squares and arrange into shallow containers.

2. Set up the tissue paper, individual bowls of glue with brushes and the cardboard tubes in a workspace with plenty of room for each child.

3. Explore and discuss the images of the animal prints with the children.

4. Rather than asking the children to simply describe the pattern, encourage their exploration with 'I wonder…?' style questions, e.g. 'I wonder why a giraffe has spots and a zebra has stripes?' and 'I wonder why each side of the moth wings are identical?'

5. Note the children's thoughts, ideas and questions for possible follow-up activity and display.

6. Share the craft materials with the children explaining that they are each going to make an animal.

7. Ask the children to think about the animals that you have talked about and others that they might know of with patterns or prints.

8. Ask them to draw a picture or simple plan of the animal that they are going to create. Annotate with ideas or, depending on stage, ask for emergent writing to be used.

9. Allow time for each child to create their animal model. Assist as required, allowing creative licence with the patterned papers!

10. Display the completed models along with the notes from discussion of the images.

What's in it for the children?

This is a creative opportunity for children to focus on discussing and describing patterns found in the animal world before creating an animal pattern of their own.

Taking it forward

- Challenge the children to invent their very own patterned creature. Provide art materials and encourage originality.

Snail trails

Pattern in the wider world

What you need:

- Talking prompts related to snails, e.g. stories, photographs, videos (optional)
- Salt dough
- Paper
- PVA glue and spreaders
- Shallow tray
- Glitter or sand

Top tip

It is much more manageable (much less messy!) to lay the paper into the shallow tray and shake the glitter from side to side than to pour glitter directly onto the paper.

What's in it for the children?

This is an interesting activity to focus learning on swirling, whirling and looping patterns. The movements and motion required to create this pattern are essential as the children move into early letter formation, and this activity can be a fun way into more focused pattern making, with fluidity for letter formation in mind.

Taking it forward

- Head outdoors to find and investigate snail trails. Plan in advance to avoid disappointment.
- Create trails on card for imaginative use with salt dough snails.
- Provide water and brushes in an outdoor space, encouraging children to use the water with the brushes to create disappearing snail trails on a much larger scale and across a variety of surfaces.

What to do:

1. Talk with the children about their knowledge of snail trails. If available, use talking prompts to stimulate discussion around appearance of trails and the movement of snails.

2. As a supplementary activity at this point; you may wish to use salt dough to create model snails with the children. Move and play with these in different directions, looping and swirling them as they create a path. Emphasise the slow movement of snails.

3. Give each child a sheet of paper and some glue in a small tub with a spreader. Fill a shallow tray, slightly larger than the paper, with glitter or sand.

4. Invite the children to use the glue with the spreader, thinking about and creating their snail trail patterns on paper. Slowly applying the glue in swirling, whirling, looping patterns is the aim during this activity.

5. Encourage them to share and compare with others. Can they see the 'invisible' pattern?

6. Once the glue has been applied, lay the paper in the shallow tray and shake gently until the trail is covered in the sand or glitter, making the pattern very visible. This may require adult support.

Sock sort

Pattern in the wider world

What you need:

- Selection of pairs of patterned children's socks
- Basket
- Washing line and pegs (optional)
- Sock-themed storybooks (optional)

Top tip ⭐

Differentiate this activity by altering the distinctiveness in pattern and colour of the socks provided. For example, a basket of all pink socks with slightly different patterns must be looked at closely; a basket filled with patterns of different colours will be easier to pair.

What's in it for the children?

Within these activities, an everyday object becomes the focus of pattern awareness as well as introducing the concepts and language of matching and pairing. Using a familiar, everyday and accessible material also provides an opportunity for children to independently extend their learning beyond the setting.

Taking it forward

- Provide sock-shaped paper templates and coloured pens or crayons. Invite the children to design a pair of socks. Create a display of the sock designs.

- Ask children to investigate socks at home. Share matching and grouping activities with parents/carers.

What to do:

1. This activity can be as simple or as challenging as you require, depending on time, focus and experience of the children.

2. Present the unpaired socks in a basket and ask the children to pair them up. Can they find a match for each sock and lay them beside each other?

3. String a washing line at child height in a safe place within the setting. Provide the basket of socks and pegs and challenge the children to hang the socks onto the line in matching pairs.

4. Alternatively, ask children to sort the socks into groups rather than pairs. Either provide examples of prompts for groups such as a spotty group, a stripy group, a single coloured group, etc. or leave it open ended and allow the children to group according to their own chosen criteria. This is great for assessment.

5. Share storybooks about socks. These often have lively illustrations of different patterned socks that stimulate lots of discussion.

Nuts and bolts

Pattern in the wider world

What you need:

- Selection of DIY hardware, e.g. nuts, bolts, washers
- Shallow basket or tray
- Salt dough
- Rolling pins

What's in it for the children?

This is an opportunity to create and explore shapes and patterns using interesting objects that may not have been handled before. The objects themselves often have weight and distinct shapes that are unique to DIY hardware, so this is an engaging and unusual opportunity. Working alongside the children, you can help to expand their use of descriptive pattern and shape-related vocabulary.

Taking it forward

- Try exploring pattern and print-making using the hardware objects with paint and paper.
- Challenge the children to use the objects to create a picture on the dough surface.

✚ Health & Safety

Ensure the hardware you present to the children is safe for them to handle. Avoid sharp or rough pieces such as screws. Think about how the children are going to work with each object. If in doubt, leave it out.

What to do:

1. Arrange the hardware pieces in the shallow basket or tray.

2. Give each child a large ball of dough and a rolling pin.

3. Demonstrate how to roll the dough into a large flat surface to work on, around 1 cm deep.

4. Allow time for the children to roll themselves a flat dough surface. Offer support and begin again where necessary.

5. Invite the children to explore the different shapes and patterns they can create on the surface of the dough by pressing, stamping, rolling, scoring and in any other way they wish.

6. Sit alongside the children as they explore, helping them to discuss and describe the different shapes and patterns being made.

7. Encourage the children to use their own descriptive vocabulary, e.g. stripy, squiggly, round, straight, as well as encouraging the language of comparison, e.g. 'My pattern is like a snail shell.'